THiS BOOK
BELONGS TO:

....

....

....

to all the children
SARAH

*to the ghost
in the lift*
LUCiA

HODDER CHILDREN'S BOOKS

First published in the United States by Little Bee Books in 2020
This edition published by Hodder and Stoughton in 2021

Text copyright © Sarah S. Brannen, 2020
Illustrations copyright © Lucia Soto, 2020

The moral rights of the author and illustrator have been asserted.
All rights reserved.

A CIP catalogue record for this book is available from
the British Library.

HB ISBN: 9781444960938
10 9 8 7 6 5 4 3 2 1
PB ISBN: 9781444960945
10 9 8 7 6 5 4 3 2 1

Printed and bound in China

MIX
Paper from
responsible sources
FSC® C104740

Hodder Children's Books
An imprint of Hachette Children's Group
Part of Hodder and Stoughton
Carmelite House
50 Victoria Embankment
London EC4Y 0DZ

An Hachette UK Company
www.hachette.co.uk
www.hachettechildrens.co.uk

UNCLE
BOBBY'S
WEDDING

SARAH S. BRANNEN
LUCIA SOTO

Hodder
Children's
Books

Bobby was Chloe's favourite uncle.

He took her rowing on the river.
He taught her the names of the stars.

Once, they even climbed
to the top of a lighthouse.
"Let's live here!" said Chloe.
"I'd like that," said Uncle Bobby.

Most of all, Chloe loved flying kites with Uncle Bobby. So when Mummy planned the first picnic of summer, Chloe was as happy as a ladybird.

Mummy and Chloe made iced tea and chicken drumsticks, banana bread and rhubarb pie. Bobby and his friend, Jamie, brought bottles of fizzy lemonade.

After pie, Uncle Bobby and Jamie made an announcement.
"We're getting married!" said Uncle Bobby.

Mummy whooped and hugged him.
Daddy shook hands with Jamie. Everyone
was smiling and talking and crying and laughing.

Everyone except . . . Chloe.

"Mummy," said Chloe, "I don't understand!
Why is Uncle Bobby getting married?"
"Bobby and Jamie love each other," said Mummy.
"When grown-up people love each other that
much, sometimes they get married."

"But," said Chloe, "Bobby is my
special uncle. I don't want him to get married."
"I think you should talk to him," said Mummy.

Chloe found Uncle Bobby sitting on a swing.
"Why do you have to get married?" she asked.
"Jamie and I want to live together and have
our own family," said Bobby.

"You want kids?"
"Only if they're just like you," said Bobby.

"That's a pretty good reason," said Chloe.

"But—" said Chloe.
"But what?" asked Uncle Bobby.
"But I still don't think you should get married.
I want us to keep having fun together like always."

"I promise we'll still have fun together," said Bobby.
"You'll always be my sweet pea."

Bobby and Jamie asked Chloe to go to the ballet with them.

Afterwards, they had milkshakes.

Jamie imitated the ballet dancers and Chloe
laughed so hard, her milkshake went up her nose.

Uncle Bobby and Jamie taught Chloe to sail.
She fell in the water at the dock, but
Jamie dove in after her.

Then Bobby jumped in, too,
and they all swam until suppertime.

At night, Chloe, Bobby and Jamie sang songs
by the campfire and toasted marshmallows.

"I wish both of you were my uncles," said Chloe.

"Well, you're getting your wish," said Jamie.
"When we get married, I'll be your uncle, too."

On the day of the wedding,
Chloe put on her new dress.

Everyone was excited and busy.

Uncle Bobby lost the rings.

Jamie couldn't tie his bow tie.

Chloe found the rings in Bobby's jacket pocket.
She helped Jamie with his tie. And she helped Mummy
put the perfect finishing touches on the wedding cake.

"We're ready!" said Chloe.

An afternoon breeze cooled the garden.
Daisies and violets bloomed in the grass and
the air smelled like roses. Cousins, grandparents
and friends watched Chloe walk down the
aisle holding a basket of flowers.

She was so happy, she felt
like doing a cartwheel. Instead,
she scattered flower petals all around.

And then Bobby and Jamie got married.

"That was the best wedding ever!" said Chloe.
"I think so, too," said Uncle Jamie.

The band started to play. Chloe jumped up and
grabbed Uncle Bobby's and Uncle Jamie's hands.
They danced until the moon rose.